I might look like a regular dog to you,

but I am really a dog from outer space.

I am from Sirius, the Dog Star.

Only dogs live on my planet,

and we are in charge of everything.

METRO-GOLDWYN-MAYER PICTURES PRESENTS A JIM HENSON PICTURES PRODUCTION "GOOD BOY!" MOLLY SHANNON LIAM AIKEN KEVIN NEALON CO-PRODUCER BILL BANNERMAN MUSIC BY MARK MOTHERSBAUGH EDITED BY CRAIG P. HERRING PRODUCTION DESIGNER JERRY WANEK DIRECTOR OF PHOTOGRAPHY JAMES GLENNON, ASC EXECUTIVE PRODUCER STEPHANIE ALLAIN PRODUCED BY LISA HENSON KRISTINE BELSON SCREEN STORY BY ZEKE RICHARDSON AND JOHN HOFFMAN SCREENPLAY BY JOHN HOFFMAN DIRECTED BY JOHN HOFFMAN ©2003 METRO-GOLDWYN-MAYER PICTURES INC. ALL RIGHTS RESERVED. DISTRIBUTED BY MGM DISTRIBUTION CO.

www.mgm.com

1 2 3 4 5 6 7 8 9 10
❖
First Edition

# GOOD BOY!

## Dog's Best Friend

Adapted by Kate Egan
Based on the screenplay by John Hoffman
Screen story by Zeke Richardson
and John Hoffman

HarperFestival®
A Division of HarperCollins*Publishers*

I came to Earth on a mission—
to see how dogs live here.

Long ago, all dogs lived on Sirius.

Then some of them traveled to Earth.

They were sent to take over the planet,

but no one on Sirius knew if they did.

The dogs never reported back.

My mission on Earth was

to find out what happened.

I was surprised by what I found.

I was also surprised by *who* I found.

I met somebody important on Earth.

I met Owen, a ten-year-old boy.

When I first met Owen,

I didn't think we would get along.

He asked me to roll over.

He asked me to fetch things.

Owen didn't understand.

Dogs from Sirius are very smart.

Dogs from Sirius do not do tricks.

Owen had never heard of my planet.

He had some bad news for me.

Owen said that dogs had not done

what they were supposed to do.

They did not take over the Earth.

They had not even tried!

I found out that most Earth dogs
are *pets*.

They let humans scratch their ears.
They let humans boss them around.

I could not believe it.

I knew one thing for sure.

I could never be anybody's pet!

I could not get home right away

because my spaceship was damaged.

For a little while,

I had to pretend I was Owen's pet.

I did not really mind it.

Before I knew it,

Owen and I became friends!

Owen gave me a new name.

He called me Hubble,

after a famous astronomer.

My name on Sirius is just

a number—3942.

I like my new name much better.

Owen rubs my belly.

No one had done that for me before.

It puts me right to sleep!

One day some kids teased me,

but Owen came to my defense.

He said it was because

dogs are "Man's best friend."

Where I come from,

dogs don't need friends.

But I like being friends with Owen.

I also like playing catch with Owen.

At first, I didn't know how

the game worked.

It took me a long time to learn to catch,

but now I am good at it.

Owen is very patient.

I also like joking around with Owen.

Owen knows I'm not supposed to

talk to humans.

He keeps my secret safe.

Owen introduced me to some other dogs.

At first, I thought they were

a little spoiled.

Dogs on Sirius do not go to beauty parlors.

Dogs on Sirius do not wear clothes.

Dogs on Sirius do not give kisses!

But I grew to like these dogs.

Owen's family moved around a lot,

so Owen was always the new kid in town.

He never fit in.

Owen was my first good friend.

I think I was his first good friend, too.

Owen's family was about to move again.

I thought I would be moving, too.

I thought I would be returning to Sirius.

Owen did not want me to leave.

He wanted to keep me as his pet.

He wanted to take me to his new home,

but Owen did not make me stay.

He was too good a friend to do that to me.

He helped me fix my radio.

Then I was able to get in touch with
the dogs from Sirius.

I went back there in a spaceship.

Do you know what I found out?

I did not want to be there anymore.

I wanted to go home.

And my home was not on Sirius anymore.

It was back on Earth with Owen.

I did something new when I came
back to Earth.

No dog on Sirius would have done it,
but I had left Sirius for good.

So I gave Owen a big, wet kiss!

Owen could not stop smiling.

Owen is a dog's best friend!